W9-BRI-838

Ring! YO?

Chris Raschka

Ink

DORLING KINDERSLEY PUBLISHING, INC.

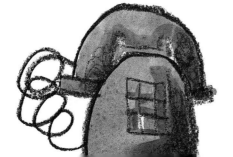

A Richard Jackson Book

Dorling Kindersley Publishing, Inc., 95 Madison Avenue, New York, New York 10016
Visit us on the World Wide Web at http://www.dk.com

Dorling Kindersley books are available at special discounts for bulk purchases for sales promotions or premiums.
Special editions, including personalized covers, excerpts of existing guides, and corporate imprints can be created in large
quantities for specific needs. For more information, contact Special Markets Dept., Dorling Kindersley Publishing, Inc.,
95 Madison Avenue, New York, New York, 10016; fax: (800) 600-9098.

Raschka, Christopher.   Ring! Yo? / Chris Raschka.—1st ed.   p. cm.   "A Richard Jackson book."
Summary: In a conversation on the telephone, two friends, one black and one white, have a disagreement and then make up.
ISBN 0-7894-2614-5   [1. Friendship—Fiction.]   I. Title. PZ7.R18141 2000 [E]—dc21   99-41080 CIP

The illustrations for this book were created using watercolor, pastels, and cut paper. Printed and bound in U.S.A.
First Edition, 2000
2   4   6   8   10   9   7   5   3   1

For Renate

Ring!

No.

And?

Um.

Then?

Yes.

See.

Hey! What just happened there?

Was it this?

Ring!

Yo?

Hi.

Hey!

Listen.

Uh huh.

Doing much?

No.

Well.

You?

Maybe.

Oh.

I might.

Mmm.

I saw you.

So.

You were with Billy.

And?

I hate Billy!

What?

I'm mad.

You are?

I am going out to play.

When?

This afternoon with Franky.

Um.

But not with you.

Why?

Because you like Billy.

So what?

That makes me mad.

Then?

You are not my friend.

No?

Understand?

Yes.

I will never play with you.

Never?

Never.

Ever?

I change my mind.

You do?

I do want to be friends.

Me too!

We will play together.

We will?

Do you want to play with me and Franky?

I do!

We can still be friends.

See?

I do like you.

See.

Bye.

See ya!

Or was it something else?